This book belongs to

....

For Mark "The Claw" Shaw — D.O.

For Arlo, Elsa and Finn — P.B.

Scholastic Canada Ltd.
604 King Street West, Toronto, Ontario M5V 1E1, Canada

Scholastic Inc.
557 Broadway, New York, NY 10012, USA

Scholastic Australia Pty Limited
PO Box 579, Gosford, NSW 2250, Australia

Scholastic New Zealand Limited
Private Bag 94407, Botany, Manukau 2163, New Zealand

Scholastic Children's Books
Euston House, 24 Eversholt Street, London NW1 1DB, UK

www.scholastic.ca

Library and Archives Canada Cataloguing in Publication

Cataloguing in publication data is available for this title.

ISBN: 978-1-4431-7549-4

First published by Scholastic New Zealand Ltd. in 2017.
This edition published by Scholastic Canada Ltd. in 2019.
Text and music copyright © 2017 by Dean O'Brien.
Illustrations copyright © 2017 by Paul Beavis.
All rights reserved.

6 5 4 3 2 1   Printed in Canada 119   19 20 21 22 23 24

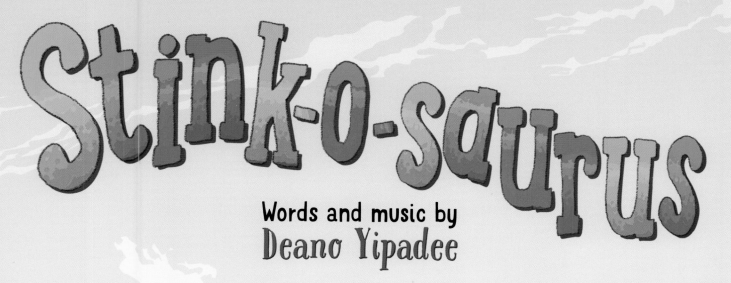

Stink-o-saurus

Words and music by
Deano Yipadee

Illustrations by
Paul Beavis

Scholastic Canada Ltd.
Toronto New York London Auckland Sydney
Mexico City New Delhi Hong Kong Buenos Aires

Long, long ago,
when dinosaurs roamed the land,
there lived a tiny little one,
whose name was Stan.

He was a rare dinosaur,
a one of a kind.
Most **roared** from their front,

his **roar** came from his behind!

When Stan asked others
to join him and play,
they groaned,
**"Not today, Stan.
Go away!"**

It was his rear-end roar
that caused such a fuss
because Stan was the very first
stink-o-saurus.

They caused
a **rumble**
from his tum,
then a sound
from his bum!

It was a noise so loud,
then out came a
whiffy cloud!

One day, Tommy T. Rex thumped into town,
gobbling up clean laundry and **kicking** houses down!

Tommy **snatched** all the candy
as the dino children cried.
Whenever he came along,
every dinosaur would hide.

As Tommy munched their goodies,
he heard a noise in the trees.

He found Stan eating 'nanas . . .
and

ROARED

him to his knees!

Startled and afraid,
Stan hid his eyes with his hands,

and his
small legs
started
shaking
in his
Stink-o-saurus
pants.

Stan tried to run fast, going

STOMP, STOMP, STOMP.

Tommy laughed behind him, going

CHOMP, CHOMP, CHOMP.

Stan leapt
behind a tree
and shrieked,
"Get away
from me!"

But as Tommy circled round,
Stan sank down to the ground.

He hid his head
between his legs,
his tail **froze**
in fear . . .

That's when out

BOOMED

that funky flame,

knocking T. Rex

on his rear!

P-f-f-f-ff-ff-t!

Forget about King Kong,
Tommy was flattened by King **PONG!**
And as he clambered to his toes,
that stink went straight into his nose.

That shaken T. Rex was so big,
but his arms were very small.
In fact, he couldn't reach his nose
to block the smell at all!

He **spluttered** and he **wobbled**
as the land began to shake,

because
Stan the Stink-o-saurus
had caused the first

EARTHQUAKE!

So Tommy T. Rex ran away,
going

THUMP, THUMP, THUMP.

Stan the hero ran behind him,
going

TRUMP, TRUMP, TRUMP!

The dinosaurs danced and hollered,

"Hip-hip HOORAY!"

for that little Stink-o-saurus
had gone and saved the day.

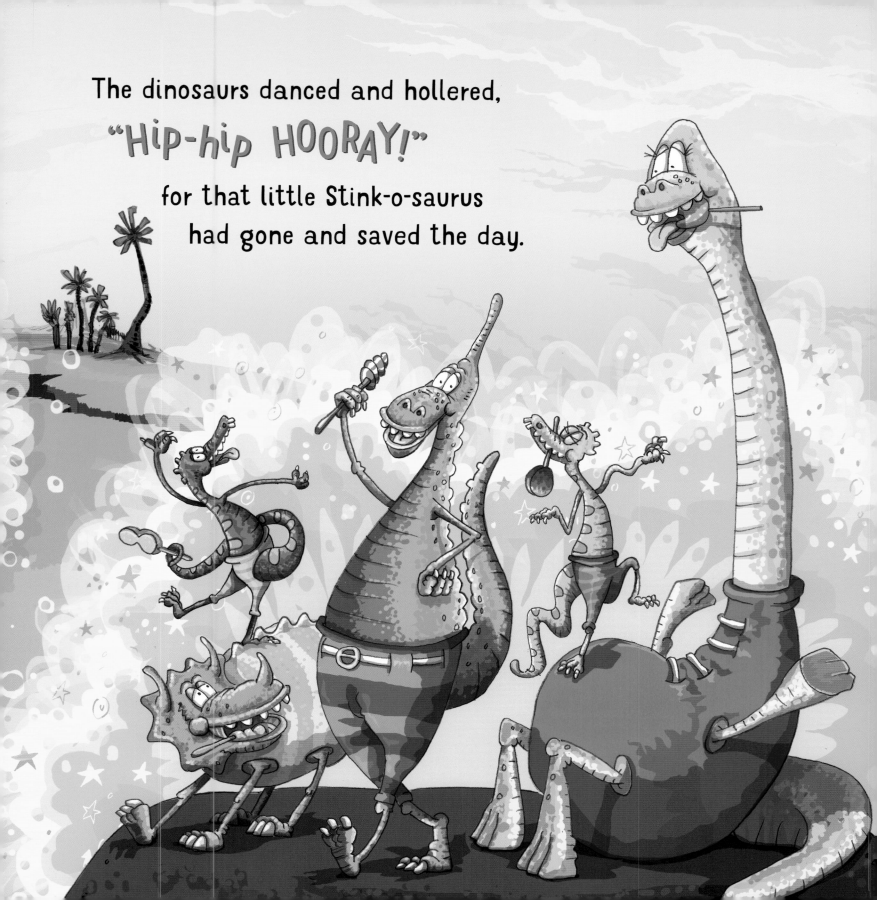

Some say it was an Ice Age that made dinosaurs extinct. Was Earth struck by a comet? Or hit by a **BIG STINK?**

But there's a chance that Stan survived . . . and hides . . . **in your underpants!**

I think that I can smell him when your noisy bottom **rants . . .**

p-f-f-f-f-f-f-f-t!

Stink-o-saurus!